Camp Cattitude

Text Copyright © 2020 by Kate Giles
Illustrations Copyright © 2020 by Ben Chandler & Enile Reiner

Dedicated to Lynne and Bill, Fai and Steven, & Jon and Michelle
with gratitude for their enthusiasm, nurture, and support,
and to sweet Bubs—for inspiration

Meowmoiselle ran Camp Cattitude, the world's top kitten camp.

She trained kittens who went on to become famous including . . .

The World's Expert Sofa Shredder,

The Olympic Napping Champion,

and The Fussiest Eater Alive.

Mother cats waited in lines to sign their kittens up for classes.

The meowy crowds drove Meowmoiselle's barky neighbors, the Rottweilers, up the wall. If the Rottweilers complained to Animal Catrol one more time, the camp would be shut down.

So when a lone kitty showed up at her door, Meowmoiselle knew she should not take in another.

But gazing at his round green eyes and stripy coat, Meowmoiselle could not resist. She enrolled him. Big mistake!

Snug was the worst behaved kitty she had ever trained.

"Kitties, let's practice ignoring our names." The other kitties like Clawdia and Meowrial ignored her perfectly.

But Snug pricked up his ears and scampered over. "Do you need any help?"

Then Snug bungled the Shedding and Shredding session.

While all the other kitties learned to make new furniture look ready for the garbage heap, Snug only scratched cat posts.

Worst of all, Snug loved everyone, even dogs.

Snug is hopeless, Meowmoiselle thought sadly after seeing him chatting up the mail mutt. How will he get by if he's this friendly? He has no cattitude. Other cats will never accept him.

One afternoon, while Meowmoiselle was at Pawsco, Snug heard caterwauling and looked outside.

The kitties had escaped into the Rottweiler's yard.

"Holy mackerel," Snug said.
"The Rottweilers will be furious!"

Snug dashed outside and darted
through the hole, bounding over
to stop them.

The kitties were making mincemeat
out of the Rottweiler's lawn chairs.

Just then, Mrs. Rottweiler leapt out, lunging towards them, snarling. "What in dog's name are you doing?"

The kitties rushed for cover . . .

under chairs, inside planters, behind dirt piles.

Except Snug. He faced her, whiskers shaking, and apologized.

Mrs. Rottweiler only drooled down at him.

His mind raced. Cattitude! Maybe cattitude could save him.

Should he scowl and turn up his nose at her?

Spit and sharpen his claws on her deck?

Yawn and lie down in her dog bed to nap?

He knew other cats would try cattitude. It was not him.

Mrs. Rottweiler steamed. He had to act now!

He saw something partially buried in a nearby planter where one of the kitties was digging a hiding hole.

A gift?

He lunged for it.

Mrs. Rottweiler's face abruptly broke into a smile. "Snakes alive! That's Mr. Rottweiler's lost bone!" She gnawed it. "Ummm. Crunchy as ever."

Snug let out a sigh of relief.

"Oh, no," they heard Meowmoiselle utter as she squeezed through the hole in the fence and saw the damage. "I'm so sorry! Are you going to complain to Animal Catrol? They'll shut us down!"

Mrs. Rottweiler hesitated, glancing at the chairs and then Snug and the bone. Snug looked around the yard. "Please give us a chance to make up for it."

Soon, Snug was directing the kitties to fix up the yard.
Meowmoiselle watched in amazed gratitude, thinking about Snug.

He was thoughtful. He was helpful. He was friendly. He wasn't at all like the famous cats she'd trained.

"You have the perfect cattitude," she told him later. "Please keep it that way." He smiled whisker-to-whisker and gave her a snug.

From that day on, Snug lived at the camp with Meowmoiselle. She taught the kitties the best of cattitude. And Snug taught them exactly what they needed to get along with each other and everyone else—grrreat meownors.

Made in the USA
Las Vegas, NV
17 March 2022

4580581 1R00017